My Father, My Companion

Happy Reading -

Geraldine Lee Susi

January 2012

*Thomas Marshall
Father*

*John Marshall
Son*

My Father, My Companion

Life at The Hollow, Chief Justice John Marshall's Boyhood Home in Virginia

Written and Illustrated by
Geraldine Lee Susi

EPM Publications
Delaplane, Virginia

Dedication

❧

For Evelyn Metzger
whose interest in The Hollow
and whose desire to know more
about the boy who became the
great Chief Justice,
inspired the writing of this story

Library of Congress Cataloging-in-Publication Data

Susi, Geraldine Lee.
  My father, my companion: life at The Hollow, Chief Justice John Marshall's boyhood home in Virginia / written and illustrated by Geraldine Lee Susi.
  p cm.
  Includes bibliographical references.
  Summary: John Marshall, who grows up to become the Chief Justice of the United States Supreme Court, spends a happy childhood with his family in 18th century Fauquier County, Virginia, enjoying a particularly close relationship with his father and teacher, Thomas Marshall.
    ISBN 1-889324-22-1 (pbk}
    1. Marshall, John, 1755-1835—Childhood and youth—Juvenile Fiction. [1. Marshall, John, 1755-1835—Childhood and youth—Fiction 2. Frontier and pioneer life—Virginia—Fauquier County—Fiction. 3. Fathers and sons—Fiction. 4. Marshall, Thomas, 1730-1802. 5. Fauquier County (Va.}—History—18th century—Fiction. 6. United States—History—18th century—Fiction.] I. Title.
  PZ7.S96565 My 2001
  [Fic]—de21

                                                                    2001042899

EPM Publications, Inc., 4138 Fox Hollow Road
  Delaplane, VA 20144
Printed in Canada

Cover and book design by Tom Huestis
Illustrations by Geraldine Lee Susi

Fauquier County in Colonial Times

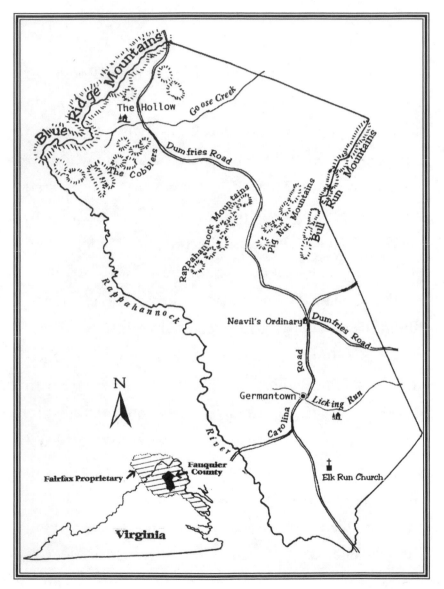

Author's Notes

*H*AVING PERSONALLY VISITED The Hollow, photographing and touching the very walls, floors and land where John Marshall lived almost two and a half centuries ago, I set about to tell his boyhood story as I envisioned it might have happened. As I conducted my research on John Marshall for this story, I discovered many inconsistencies in information from one author to another. There was also relatively little information about John Marshall as a young boy. When writing I tried to remain as true as possible to the facts that I found, especially with respect to any primary sources that I came upon. However, when there were conflicting dates, I chose those that made the most sense with all other sources. Where no information was available, I took the liberty of inventing those events which I imagined might have taken place. John Marshall's family was fascinating. They were strong, hearty, exceedingly intelligent people, ahead of their times in educating women; and they contributed greatly to all levels of government—county(Fauquier), state (Virginia), and national (The United States). Although in this story I chose to focus primarily on John Marshall's formative years, particularly those spent at The Hollow, it is important to remember that he was a man who served in many capacities: soldier in the Revolutionary War; lawyer; diplomat; Congressman; U.S.Secretary of State; and the longest serving Chief Justice of the U.S.Supreme Court, holding that position from 1801 until 1835. There is an abundance of books which delve into the adult life of John Marshall, written by noted historians and judicial experts. I direct readers who wish to know this side of John Marshall to look to these very learned sources. For my initial outline I used the following excerpt from a brief autobiography, then fleshed it out using my imagination aided by my research:

"I was born," Marshall wrote, *"on the 24th of September, 1755 in the County of Fauquier, at that time one of the frontier counties of Virginia. My father possessed scarcely any fortune, and had received a very limited education, but was a man to whom nature had been bountiful, and who had*

assiduously improved her gifts. He superintended my education and gave me an early taste for history and poetry. At the age of twelve, I had transcribed Pope's Essay on Man, with some of his Moral Essays.

"There being no grammar school in that part of the country in which my father resided, I was sent, at fourteen, about one hundred miles from my home, to be placed under the tuition of Mr. Campbell, a clergyman of great respectability. I remained with him one year, after which I was brought home and placed under the care of a Scotch gentleman who was just introduced into the parish as Pastor, and who resided in my father's family. He remained in the family one year, at the expiration of which time I had commenced reading Horace and Livy. I continued my studies with no other aid than my dictionary. My father superintended the English part of my education, and to his care I am indebted for anything valuable which I may have acquired in my youth. He was my only intelligent companion; and was both a watchful parent and an affectionate friend. The young men within my reach were entirely uncultivated; and the time I passed with them was devoted to hardy athletic exercises."

John Marshall, *at age 72, writing to his friend,* Joseph Story

Chief Justice of the
United States Supreme Court

John Marshall

Fond Memories

THE DISTINGUISHED white-haired old man gazed wistfully out the parlor window at the children frolicking on the soft, green, grassy slopes. Well into his seventies now, John Marshall was still a handsome man by anyone's standards. Watching his sons play with his grandchildren and his nieces and nephews — all racing and playing tag, filling the summer air with giggles and joyful squeals—set him to remembering the carefree days of his own childhood with his father. His earliest memories dated from the time he was a small boy on Licking Run in the southern part of Fauquier County, then still part of Prince William County. His favorite memories though were always of his youthful days spent at The Hollow in the northern part of Fauquier County, just a short distance from where he was now standing at The Oaks, the last home his father had built in Virginia. Thomas Marshall had provided well for his children, all fifteen of them. "My father did an admirable job", the Chief Justice of the United States thought to himself. "Everything I am today I owe to him."

The old man turned from the window and walked across the parlor. He settled himself into a comfortable chair, stretched out his long legs in front of him, leaned back and closed his eyes. With the laughter of the children playing in his ears like a pleasant lullaby, he dozed off remembering the days of his youth as old people are often apt to do.

A Carefree Child

"BE CAREFUL, THOMAS. He's still just a child," the mother admonished as she handed the little boy up to his father. John was her first-born, and only son.

"Don't worry, Mary. He needs to learn to sit tall in the saddle if he's going to get along in these woods and meadows. A surveyor has to ride long and far. I want John to be able to come along with me someday." Mary was reassured as she watched her husband gently place their son on the saddle and snuggle him up against his own body. Thomas Marshall then carefully nudged the gray horse forward. The boy sat straight and tall as the air began to rustle his thick, auburn hair, and his dark eyes sparkled with excitement. In his

father's protective grasp, he knew he had nothing to fear.

"Faster, Father, faster," the child urged laughing with glee. Already he was eager to feel the wind in his face and to race to far off places. Thomas was pleased that his young son was ready to test his wings and fly like a daring fledgling.

But the ride that day went only as far as the fields and gardens surrounding the house and down to Licking Run. They returned much too soon to suit the little boy. "Don't go home, Father" he begged. "Ride more."

"Enough for today, John. Your mother will scold me if we stay away too long."

"See, Mary, I told you he would love it," Father said as he tried to hand the child back to his mother waiting impatiently at the front door. John tried desperately to cling to the saddle, but his father's reach was much longer than his, and he lifted the boy into the air and down into the anxious arms of his mother. Thomas Marshall was thrilled that his son showed no fear and wanted to continue his ride. He knew John would grow to be a wonderful companion for him on the trips that lay ahead.

John's mother set him down, and as soon as his little feet touched the ground, he was off and running, chasing the chickens around the yard and racing through the garden. The louder the chickens squawked, the harder John chased them and his laughter echoed through the yard. He was at his happiest when he was free and racing like the wind. Those days in the little wooden cabin near Licking Run were carefree ones for John. He was the first child, but he would definitely not be the last.

Thomas Marshall had chosen well when he married seventeen-year-old Mary Randolph Isham Keith. She was strong, intelligent, well-educated as the daughter of a minister, and she was related to some of the most important families of Virginia. Those family names, not only Randolph and Isham, but also Jefferson and Lee, would open many doors for the Marshall family throughout their lives and keep them in the best of company.

Thomas Marshall was a surveyor by profession, and as such often had to leave his growing family to go on trips into the wilderness. At these times John would cry to go along, promising, "But I will be good, Father. I want to go with you."

His father would hoist him up on his horse, give him a hug and say, "Someday, John, you will be big enough to come with me. And when you are, I promise I will take you." And John would watch his father ride off to survey the unsettled lands to the west until he could no longer see him in the distance.

Early in his life, Thomas Marshall's friend and workmate was George Washington who, at the age of sixteen, was employed by Thomas, the Sixth Lord Fairfax. Lord Fairfax, proprietor of a vast English land grant in Virginia, spent much of his life on a manor beyond the Blue Ridge Mountains enjoying the excellent hunting and fishing that it afforded him. Since his land grant was well over five million acres, Lord Fairfax hired young George to survey and divide huge unsettled sections of his land into parcels. These surveyed lots would then be available to people seeking such grants of land. During this time, Washington and Marshall took advantage of every opportunity to meet and share tales of their latest exploits. Neither one realized then the many parallel paths their friendship would take them on in determining the future of colonial America.

George and Thomas had grown up together in

Westmoreland County located in the Virginia lowlands between the Rappahannock and the Potomac Rivers. Although the Washington family owned a large plantation with many slaves, and the Marshalls had a much smaller farm with few slaves, still the two boys had gone to school together and been best friends. They also shared a common interest in surveying, particularly surveying in the sparsely settled frontier lands of colonial Virginia. Those experiences with George Washington had established Thomas Marshall's career as a surveyor, and thus would provide him and his family with many benefits in the future.

Thomas's father died in 1752 and, as the oldest son, he inherited the family's farm on Mattox Creek. Thomas, however, decided to sell the 200 acres of low, marshy land, since it had long ago been worn out by too many years of tobacco planting. Through his job as surveyor, he knew there was beautiful, fertile land and many opportunities to be had in the western part of Virginia. He convinced his widowed mother, Elizabeth Markham Marshall, and his younger brothers and sisters to come with him. So with all their family possessions they set off.

Living at Licking Run

*T*HOMAS KNEW OF AN AREA that had been settled earlier by a group of German miners along
Licking Run. There was a house, small but well built,
that would serve them well, at a cost within their
financial means. Soon after settling there, he had the
good fortune to meet the Reverend James Keith's
daughter. After a brief courtship, they were married
and he brought Mary to live at Licking Run. It was
there on the 24th of September, 1755 that their first
child, John, was born.

Young John loved the little Germantown house.
The two rooms downstairs were very small, but cozy,
with a fireplace at either end and there was a small loft
upstairs. His parents and their growing family shared
this space along with Grandmother Marshall, and it
served them well. They had a few small outbuildings:
a kitchen, a smokehouse, and another which served as
the quarters for their family slaves. Some of the slaves
had been with the Marshall family since their days in
Westmoreland County. They helped tend the crops
and care for the animals. In fact, for years old Joe and

Bett had served Grandmother and now they also helped John's mother in the house. The work was shared by Hannah and Jacob and several other slaves who had been willed to Thomas by his father. Such helping hands were most welcome because as John grew up, he never remembered a time that his mother did not have a baby in her arms or wasn't expecting the birth of one. At the age of one, John was joined by his sister, Elizabeth, and a year after that by sister Mary Ann. Grandmother Marshall was there to hold and rock each of her grandbabies. Thomas and Mary Marshall considered themselves fortunate to have her and her loving help with them for so many years.

In the Spring and Summer and Fall, John loved to be outdoors running and jumping and fishing and riding. When the winter winds began to blow and the snow began to fall, the house was cozy and warm and their activities moved inside. Winter was a special time because his mother would not only rock the babies, but she would read to them from the Bible or from another one of the precious books that she and her husband owned. From very early on, John's mother and father shared their love for reading and for books with their children. John loved to hear his mother's voice as she read aloud, and he learned as he listened. Later in life, John would be very proud of his mother's education. Many men at that time could not read or write and certainly very few women could.

John's youthful days at Licking Run passed very quickly, for young children are often too self absorbed to know or even care about all that is going on around them. John did remember, though, the day when his father came home excited with the news that they finally were to become part of the new county of Fauquier. It would be carved out of what was then Prince William County and they, the Marshalls, were living right in the heart of it. Thomas Marshall declared that he intended to play an important part in developing this county. After all he had been survey-ing this area for years now and knew it as well or bet-ter than most men.

Shortly after that news John's father came home one day and, lifting the almost five-year-old into his arms, announced, "You are now the son of a Justice of the Peace of the County of Fauquier." Then turning to his wife he continued, "And you are the wife of the newly appointed County Surveyor." Everyone had been so excited and happy that day. John wasn't sure what a justice of the peace was, but he knew it must be something important for it made Mother and Father and Grandmother happy. Later he would learn that justice of the peace was not only an important position, but very respected as well. There were only twelve men in the whole county chosen to serve in this capacity. They had a great deal of power and as a group served as the county court with authority to settle all civil and property disputes. They had to make sure that the county abided by the rules set by the House of Burgesses in Williamsburg, the most important colonial governing group. In addition, every two years the sheriff of the county was selected from among these twelve men. Serving in both capacities made Thomas Marshall a well-known figure throughout the county. These were rewarding but busy times for him.

While his father was traveling about the county, John continued to grow and mature enjoying a comfortable and happy life at Licking Run. Like his father, he was tall and his outdoor activities made him robust and hardy. As the oldest child, he was the natural leader of his little sisters. Because of his good nature, his two sisters adored him. But when his father announced that he finally had a baby brother, little Thomas, John's life at age five, took on new excitements.

A Better Place

As THE CHILDREN GREW, the dinner hour became a lively time for discussion and learning. When Father was at home discussions were always interesting for he caught everyone up on the latest news of the county and the colony. The children would listen as Father and Mother and Grandmother discussed the events of the day. As they got older, they were given opportunities to ask questions and eventually they could voice their own opinions.

It was at one such dinner conversation that Father announced, "Mary, I've found a wonderful piece of land in the northern part of the county on a hillside near a branch of Goose Creek. It will be a much better place for our growing family. I would like to build us a new house there. I will make it larger than this house and we'll have ever so much more land. I'm sure that all of you will think it is as wonderful as I do once you see it. In surveying it, I've determined a marvelous location for the house in a sort of hollow completely surrounded by mountains."

Everyone began to ask questions at once, and Father said, "Everyone shall have a turn to talk. Grandmother as the eldest shall go first and then on down the line."

"Thomas, will there be space for me at this new home, and will I continue to stay with you?" Grandmother wanted to know.

"Of course, there will be room for you and I hope you will always stay with our family for as long as you live." And Grandmother was pleased with that answer.

Mother asked, "Have you drawn up plans for the house yet? How big do you think it will be?"

"I have been thinking a great deal about what the house should be like," he responded. "I think that you will agree that it should definitely be bigger than this one to provide for our growing family. There are many huge oaks growing nearby that can be milled into strong boards and beams. There is also plenty of natural stone for fireplaces, and we'll have one at each end of the house. I will take Ben and Jacob and Caesar with me and we will begin construction as soon as the weather allows. I welcome your thoughts on anything else that we should include."

"I think that sounds wonderful, Thomas, and it will be so nice to have a home that was built just for us. I'm sure you will see to it that it is perfect for us."

In his turn, John asked, "Father, are there fields to run in and streams to fish in like there are here?"

"John, the fields are rich and green and the mountains are full of game of all sorts. Goose Creek passes through our land and has more fish than Licking Run ever had. You will have much there to keep you busy."

Elizabeth just wanted to be assured that no one would be left behind. Mary Ann and Thomas were too busy eating their bread pudding to ask anything. They were still too young to realize what Father's announcement meant.

And so it was that after that evening, they all began to call the new place "The Hollow". John was not too sure about the move. Germantown and Licking Run had been the only home he'd ever known. He didn't really want to go someplace new. Mother and Grandmother, however, were most pleased with the news, and his sisters and brother didn't really seem to have any opinions of their own.

As the construction of the house slowly progressed, John soon found himself as excited about its possibilities as everyone else. Each time that Father would return from a trip up to The Hollow, everyone would be anxious to hear the latest details about what had been completed. John began to be as anxious as his mother to see it, and before he knew it, it was time to begin preparing for the move. There was so much to be done and everyone would have to help.

A Difficult Move

WHEN THE BIG DAY TO MOVE finally arrived, Father and the servants had disassembled the furniture, rolled up the feather beds, packed the pewter and china, and loaded all their possessions into several large, wooden wagons. Grandmother and Mother, his sisters, Elizabeth and Mary Ann, and little Thomas would ride in one of the carriages. John, now almost nine, was allowed to ride on one of the horses beside his father. The livestock was tied behind the wagons and some of it had been brought on ahead during father's previous trips. But the bulk of what they owned was packed and bundled onto this caravan. The family servants would drive the wagons and help with many other duties along the way. Father said it would probably take several days to get to The Hollow barring any unforeseen accidents or bad weather. As such this would be the longest journey any of the children had ever been on.

As they moved out onto their rutted dirt lane to get onto the Carolina Road, John glanced back over his shoulder one last time at the only home he'd known since he was born. He whispered a quick farewell, then nudged his horse with his heel and galloped off. It was time to look forward to a new start and new adventures.

"Father, will anyone live in this house now that we are not there any longer?" he asked as he reined in his horse beside his father's.

"Don't worry, John. The house will not be empty long. John Ariss and his wife have agreed to pay us the sum of 250 pounds to acquire this property. They will probably settle in here just as soon as we are gone. We will use that money to pay for our rights to the property at The Hollow. I know that you are going to like our new home every bit as much as I do. But now we must see to it that the wagons and the ladies and children are cared for on this journey. I'll need your help, for there will probably be some very difficult moments along the way. Traveling this country alone on horseback is much simpler than trying to move wagons weighted down with our life's possessions. These roads are not the best for such purposes. They are intended to be used for getting tobacco and goods to market, not really for carriages with riders."

Father had decided that the best route for them to take would be to go north on the Carolina Road to George Neavil's Ordinary. From there they would go northwesterly on the upper branch of Dumfries Road to Bethel through the thoroughfare of the Rappahannock Mountains, and then north by the foot of the Cobbler Mountains until finally reaching The Hollow. Father knew this route well since he and George Washington had traveled it often going to Lord Fairfax's Greenway Court Manor while on surveying trips. However, describing this route was a much simpler task than accomplishing it, as John was soon to discover. It was a mere twenty-five miles or so as the crow flies, but when one had to travel along the few poorly maintained roads of the time, the distance was closer to double that. The overloaded wagons jostled and creaked as they jarred along at an agonizingly slow pace. John, who had become quite an accomplished rider since that day long ago when he rode with his father around the house at Licking Run, found himself doubling back on his chestnut mare over and over in order to stay with the wagons. Father occasionally let seven-year-old Elizabeth and six-year-old Mary Ann take turns riding on the horse with him to keep them from whining to Mother in the carriage. He had to stop frequently to rest both animals and riders.

It was early September and the maples glowed a brilliant orange. Nestled among the russet oaks and golden hickories, they painted a colorful backdrop for the travelers. The weather was pleasant and in spite of having to ford several small runs or streams, the travelers were able to move right along. At first they crossed mostly gentle, rolling hillsides, but eventually the way became steeper as the road wound up to and between the Rappahannock and Pig Nut Mountains. The incline slowed their pace and the animals began straining to pull their heavy loads. Father pulled up his horse beside the carriage and reassured the women, "Just a bit farther and we will arrive at Joseph Neavil's Ordinary where we'll stay for the night."

Thomas Marshall had stayed at many ordinaries, a type of inn, in the course of performing his duties as surveyor and justice of the peace. But it would be a new experience to do so with his whole family along. John was excited as they approached their destination. "Father, what is an ordinary like? Where will we sleep? What will we eat? Who will we see?"

"Whoa, son. Not so fast. Let me explain. An ordinary is a private home that provides travelers with food, lodging and stables for a fee. The owner of the ordinary lives there as well. We will eat at the ordinary table along with Mr. Neavil's family whenever they sit down to eat. That's why we need to stop early enough to be sure that we are there when dinner is served. There may also be other travelers staying with us as well, but we won't know that until we get there. We will pay to use the beds for the night and they will also provide a stable and pasturage for our animals. Tomorrow we will be off again early in the morning. I hope that we will be able to reach The Hollow by tomorrow night. This journey with all our belongings is taking longer than I imagined."

John glanced up ahead as he rode along beside his father. They were approaching a large house with a long front porch. Father said, "There it is, Mary. Neavil's Ordinary. I know that you and Mother and the children will be glad for the rest and food."

"I don't mean to complain, Thomas," she answered, "but these roads make for a very difficult ride. Mother Marshall, I know that you, too, are as glad as I am to see an end to this day's journey." Grandmother just nodded her head because little Thomas was fast asleep in her lap. The carriage pulled to a stop, and everyone breathed a sigh of relief.

John tied his horse to the hitching post and climbed up the wooden steps to the porch. The wall beside the front door was plastered with all sorts of papers and advertisements. He tried to read as many as he could. Several described horses that were for sale, or ones that had been stolen and many, it seemed, were about taxes. One notice gave the name of a new doctor who had just settled in the area. John wished he had more time to read them all, but he couldn't really understand everything he read. John's father shook hands with Mr. Neavil and it was obvious that they had met many times before. The two men went inside and everyone followed.

That evening at supper, John ate every bite of the venison stew and cornbread placed before him. Everyone seemed to have an appetite after the long day on the road. After they ate they were shown to their quarters, the women and children in one room and John and his father in another. Though there were several beds in the room, John slept in a trundle pulled from beneath his father's bed. He was so tired that as soon as he lay down, he fell asleep. But in the middle of the night he awoke to the sound of loud snoring. In the dim light he realized that there were now other people sleeping in the room with them. Several other travelers must have arrived later in the night. John wondered how his father managed to sleep on his trips with all these strange noises. He lay there for a while listening to the droning and eventually he fell back to sleep.

More Difficulties

THE NEXT MORNING after a breakfast of ham, eggs, porridge and coffee, the Marshalls climbed back on their horses and wagons and began the next leg of their journey. The road was definitely getting steeper as they traveled between the Pig Nut and Rappahannock Mountains. Fortunately, the horses and oxen were fresh from a good night's rest. The countryside was dotted with lovely meadows and the mountains were dense with autumn foliage. John and his father were leading the way when they heard a loud CR-A-A-CK followed by screams and children crying.

Father wheeled his horse around and galloped back in the direction of the sound and John followed quickly behind. The ladies' carriage had tipped over onto the side of the road and Mother, Grandmother and the children were all lying in a heap on top of each other. The loud cries of the children rose up from the pile. Father quickly dismounted and helped Grandmother and Mother to their feet making sure that they were all right. John jumped down and tried to calm Elizabeth and Mary Ann who seemed to be fine, only badly shaken and screaming loudly. But where was his little brother? John looked around anxiously. Suddenly he spotted the little boy down in the gully by the side of the road. John raced to him, slipping and sliding down the slope as he went. His brother was covered with dirt and leaves and he wasn't moving at all. John bent down and carefully picked him up. Cradling the child in his arms, he climbed back up the hill. When he got to the top, he could see concern and fear in each waiting face. Mother and Father immediately hurried to help him. Mother spread her shawl on the ground and they lowered the lifeless toddler down on top of it. All held their breaths as they watched. Elizabeth, who had finally stopped crying, now began to wail again and Mary Ann joined in too. Grandmother tried to hug them and calm them down, but their wailing continued. Father and Mother gently stroked the little boy's face, brushing back the hair from his forehead. They looked worriedly at one another and it seemed as though an eternity passed before their littlest boy finally began to cry. Everyone let out a sigh of relief for they had feared the worst. Mother picked Thomas up and held him tight, rocking and soothing him and reassuring him that everything would be all right. Once he calmed down she was able to see that he had suffered a nasty bump on his head, but otherwise seemed fine.

Father then made sure everyone was safely seated on a large rock by the side of the road, before he went back to survey the damage to the carriage. One of the wheels had become wedged between two rocks and snapped the axle. Caesar, Joe and Juba, the Negroes who had been driving the other wagons, were already righting the carriage and checking to see what needed to be done.

"Do we have another axle on one of the wagons?" Father asked. Joe, the oldest man, nodded his head and headed back to his wagon. He began to dig through all the stuff loaded on his wagon and finally uncovered a spare axle. He put it on his shoulder and returned to the broken carriage. Fixing an axle would not be easy to accomplish on the road like this, but they had no choice. The three men set to work with Father supervising.

Meanwhile the children took advantage of the opportunity to run and play in the grassy field. Mother and Grandmother had checked each child over carefully to be sure that no one else had been hurt in the mishap. Little Thomas seemed to be back to his busy self in spite of the bump on his head. Bett, Esther, Hannah and Jenny had come running from their wagons after the crash to help the women and children. They saw to the comfort of the two Marshall ladies and looked after the children until the carriage was repaired.

Finally the job was completed and everyone climbed back into the wagons to continue on their way. Father helped Grandmother and Mother back into the carriage and helped settle the children. He set little Thomas carefully between the two ladies and said, "You stay close to Mother. You gave us quite a scare back there, young man. We don't want anything else to happen to you." Then to his wife and mother he said, "The wagon is all fixed and is better than before. I know these roads are not very good for travel, but I assure you that our final destination will be worth it. You'll see. It should not take us too much longer."

Once again the caravan began to climb through the Pig Nut and Rappahannock Mountains. Eventually they turned west leaving those mountains behind them. But as they headed into the setting sun, the silhouette of the Blue Ridge Mountains rose up before them. This countryside was definitely hillier and rockier than what they had been used to at Germantown.

The axle repair had taken so much time that father realized they could not possibly reach their destination tonight. They would have to stay at another ordinary this evening. But at least they were all alive and well. Tomorrow they should reach The Hollow.

The next morning, after a much needed rest, they resumed their journey on the Dumfries Road winding along the Cobbler Mountains. Although the road was very rocky and rough, they rumbled along without further mishap. At last they came upon Goose Creek. It was a lovely, meandering creek, wide, but fairly shallow at this point. It was here that they would have to leave the main road and ford the creek to make their way to The Hollow. Everyone except the drivers had to step down and wait on the bank until the wagons were safely maneuvered to the other side. The horses and oxen had difficulty keeping their footing on the slippery rocks. John watched anxiously as each wagon clattered and groaned across the creek. At last all of the wagons and carriages stood on the other side.

Then, one by one, Father and John took each of the women and children to the other side on their horses. From here on the road was little more than two dirt ruts along the ground. Though this would be the last part of the journey. John was beginning to wonder if any new house could be worth so much trouble.

It was now late afternoon and the sun was descending towards the Blue Ridge, as the wagons came up from the lowland along Goose Creek. Cresting the hill, the wagons all stopped behind Father and everyone took in the breathtaking view ahead. John drew in a deep breath and looked over at his father. "You are right, Father. This is the most beautiful place. I know I'm going to love it here already."

"Welcome to The Hollow"

THERE BEFORE THEM stood their new home. Situated on a grassy knoll, the wooden frame house was surrounded on all sides by stately mountains ablaze with autumn colors. Rising directly behind the house was Naked Mountain, to the West were the stately, serene Blue Ridge Mountains, and in front of the house rose Red Oak Mountain. When everyone had had time enough to take in the beauty around them, Father announced, "Welcome to The Hollow."

The wagons pulled up to the house and Father came over to help Mother and Grandmother down from the carriage. "Joe, Juba and Caesar," he said, "see that the animals are tended to and the wagons are unloaded. Show Esther and Hannah and the others to the kitchen and let's get this house in order." The Negro servants would live in separate outbuildings behind the house which included the kitchen. There was also a stone meat house, a spring house, a stable for Father's horses and sheds for the wagons and carriages.

Then to Grandmother and Mother he said, "Come inside, ladies, and survey your new home," and he guided them to the front door. "John, girls, come see where you will be living." With that, there began a frantic bustle of activity. They climbed the stone steps and opened the front door. They entered the main room which was twice as big as the one they had left at Licking Run. It had the warm aroma of newly milled oak. Elizabeth and Mary Ann turned in circles looking at the tall ceilings. A large stone fireplace dominated the west wall of the room. Father took Mother by the hand through a door into a slightly smaller room to the east which also had a fireplace. Mother exclaimed, "Oh, Thomas, this is a lovely house. You have done a wonderful job in building it."

Father then accompanied the children to a boxed-in staircase which led upstairs. There in the loft were two rooms of very comfortable size. "Look," Father said, "there is a room for the girls and one for the boys and each room has a window." For three adults and four children this would be a very adequate and spacious house. As the furniture was gradually moved inside, Mother and Grandmother directed the placement of each piece. The beds were set up first and the feather covers unrolled and put in place. Everything was unloaded and in spite of all the unpacked boxes, it was starting to look like their own house again.

That night, Thomas and Mary Marshall sat by the fireplace and Grandmother joined them in her favorite rocking chair. The children gathered around and Father read to them from one of his favorite poetry books. John looked at the faces of his family glowing in the golden firelight. His little brother, Thomas,

was sound asleep in Grandmother's arms, Elizabeth sat on Father's lap, while Mary snuggled on Mother's lap. John was content as he sat on the floor and listened to his father's deep voice repeating lines from Shakespeare's sonnets. John thought how lucky he was. His father had built them a beautiful new home in the wilds of Fauquier County. He was an important man in the county and the future was exciting. This was a wonderful place and he was going to like living here. He hoped he could stay forever.

John would remain here for no more than ten years, but those would be ten important years in the formation of his character and personality.

Lessons at Home

ONCE THEY WERE SETTLED in at The Hollow, Mother was able to spend more time with the education of the children. Each day, she would spend time in lessons with them. As a delegate to the House of Burgesses, Father was often away in Williamsburg sitting alongside his friend and fellow delegate George Washington. Yet whenever Father was home, he would supervise the lessons of the older children which always included John. In turn, John, as the oldest, would read with his younger sisters. Grandmother, assisted by Old Hannah, would tend to the littlest ones, for child number five arrived not long after the family was settled in. He was named James Markham, after Grandmother Marshall's family name.

John loved living at The Hollow. He spent many happy hours fishing in Goose Creek. Sometimes he would just sit on the bank skipping stones, while at other times he would race along the edge leaping from rock to rock. In the spring and summer, he and his sisters picked buckets of wild berries. In the fall, they romped through the woods filling their baskets with the chestnuts that grew so abundantly there. The lush forests were alive with deer, turkey, foxes, raccoons, opossums, and squirrels. Even a bear or two came nosing around in search of something tasty to eat.

As soon as John was old enough, his father taught him how to load and shoot the long gun. John was a fast learner and soon became a skilled marksman. Being able to use a gun was an important skill when you lived on the frontier like this. He made sure that there was always plenty of fresh meat for their table. Also, with Father frequently away on business, someone would have to be able to ward off any menacing bears. Indians were once a problem in these parts. However, with the end of the French and Indian War, the British government issued the Proclamation of 1763 which provided for troops to be posted along the whole Appalachian frontier. Though they said it was for protection from the Indians, Father and George Washington, then *Colonel* Washington, agreed that it was really intended to keep anyone from moving onto lands farther to the west. In defiance of this proclamation, Col. Washington continued to survey claims to western lands.

The dinner hour continued to be the Marshall family's time for lively discussion on any number of subjects. In addition to talking about his disapproval of British policies towards the settling of land west of the mountains, Father had even bigger concerns with the tariffs or taxes being placed on the colonists. One particular evening discussion occurred after the British Parliament issued the Stamp Act. John could tell that his father was upset. "It's bad enough that England wants to tax our imports of sugar, coffee and molasses,

but now they want to tax us on every piece of paper that is printed. I won't have it, I tell you. They have no right to do this to us."

"But, Thomas," Mother replied, "what choice do we have? The King expects us to do our duty."

"King George III can try to control our imports, but this is a direct tax. Why I just heard that Patrick Henry, who can always stir up a fuss, argued quite forcefully that only the House of Burgesses with our own representatives can tax Virginians. I agree whole-heartedly."

"But, Father, what can we do about it?" John asked. "We have always done what the King and Parliament have told us to do."

"You're right, John. Perhaps it is time for us to consider a new course of action here in the colonies." John thought about that as he went to bed that night. He was old enough to realize that there was a much bigger world beyond The Hollow. And there were many things occurring in that world that could have a definite effect on his future life here. He could tell that his father was troubled and that, in turn, troubled John.

Learning By Example

*A*S OFTEN AS POSSIBLE, John accompanied his father on his rounds as justice of the peace. John especially liked those days when his father presided over the court. In addition to learning about his father's work, John also learned about Fauquier County and its citizens. He realized that many of the men looked up to his father. Not only was his father a big man, physically strong and powerful, but he was also very intelligent. The men listened carefully when he spoke, particularly when he described the events that followed Parliament's issuing of the Stamp Act. At one gathering, John heard his father report, "Many of

surveyor's chain

the merchants in the colonies decided not to import or sell any British goods. Our colonial merchants felt this would demonstrate most forcefully our displeasure with that hated act. They knew that when British merchants in the colonies began to lose money, they would quickly convince Parliament to repeal the Stamp Act. That is exactly what happened and so we Americans won our point on that issue. Unfortunately though, Parliament was not about to give up. They declared that because the colonies are under their rule, they, Parliament, could pass any laws that they decided were necessary to keep us under their control." Talking among themselves afterward, the men agreed that this should not be allowed to happen. John could tell that these men as well as his father were becoming more and more displeased with their status as colonists.

It was also during the trips with his father that John was able to meet some of the other young boys living in the area. John was growing very tall, and his long legs were a great asset. Whenever he got together with other boys they would have races to see who could run the fastest or contests to see who could jump the highest fence. More often than not John was the

Quoits

winner. But for all his athletic skill, he was not a boastful person. He let his actions speak to his ability, and as a result he was well liked and respected by his friends.

John and his father talked about all sorts of things as they rode along, and his father used these opportunities to instruct him in many areas. He taught him to recognize and name all the trees they saw. This was important for surveyors since property lines were marked and noted by the largest trees that grew along these lines particularly at the corners. John could point out the various oaks, black, white and red, as well as hickories, maples, chestnuts, sweet gums and many others. On these trips, John would carry his father's surveying equipment, which included the chains for measuring and the compasses. He learned how property was measured in poles and chains, with 25 links being a pole and four poles equaling one chain. All of this was necessary knowledge if John wanted to follow in his father's footsteps and become a surveyor. Most important, however, throughout this time, was the growth of the bond between father and son. John came to think of his father as even more than his parent and teacher. He was his best companion.

The Growing Family

JAMES MARKHAM was two when the next sister, Judith, was born. There were now three boys and three girls. Although Elizabeth and Mary were John's reading and writing companions, little Thomas, six years younger than John, became his shadow, following him everywhere and trying to copy his every move. John was flattered and enjoyed the chance to teach him outdoor games and skills. Father set up a spot not too far from the house where the boys could play at quoits. John liked to play against his father, but he decided to teach young Thomas how to play so he would have some competition when Father was away.

At first the little boy struggled with the quoits, trying as hard as he could to make some points. John watched as the little boy tried to throw the weighty metal rings at the hobs or stakes set some 20 yards apart. John allowed his brother to stand closer to the hob to give him an advantage. Although John laughed heartily at Thomas' feeble attempts, he often would have flashbacks to that scary moment when he picked up his brother's lifeless body from the bottom of the gully. He surely was thankful Thomas had not been seriously hurt that day. While John was teaching Thomas how to play quoits, his own skill at ringing the hobs increased. Soon John was able to beat even his father at the game. It was a sport that John enjoyed immensely and would continue to enjoy and excel at throughout his life.

Shortly after John's twelfth birthday, it was obvious that his mother was again expecting a baby. But this time everyone, especially Father and Grandmother, seemed very concerned. Mother was extremely tired and as a result their lessons tended to be very short. Sometimes Mother was just too tired to

have them at all. That was not like her. Then one cold January morning, Grandmother called Old Hannah to come help her. She told Bett and Esther to take all the children down to the kitchen for a while. Grandmother and Hannah disappeared into the bedroom with Mother. Father waited in the front room.

John was very concerned because he could tell that his father was worried. It seemed an interminably long time before Father finally sent word that the children should return to the house. When they came into the main room, Grandmother was holding the new baby. Father didn't say anything, he just stood there staring at the bedroom door. Why didn't Father tell them how Mother was, John wondered. John was getting more upset at his father's silence. Just as he was about to ask him how Mother was, Old Hannah came in carrying another baby. John looked from Grandmother to Old Hannah and back to Father with a look of total confusion on his face.

Then Father stepped forward and said, "Children, I want you to meet your newest little brothers." Looking at the baby in Grandmother's arms, he said, "This is William. And this is Charles," he said as he touched the baby in Old Hannah's arms. "Your mother is very, very tired, but she is doing just fine. She has outdone herself this time by presenting us with twin boys."

Elizabeth and Mary Ann, now ten and nine, jumped up and down with glee. "Look, there is a baby for you to hold and one for me to hold," Elizabeth exclaimed to her younger sister as the two girls went over to inspect the new arrivals. Father took John aside and said, "Your mother needs some time to rest and will be very busy with the care of the new babies. You can help her if you will see to the girls' and Thomas's lessons for a while. I will try to spend as much time in your instruction as I can. There is nothing more important than the education of one's mind. More than anything I want to be sure that all of my children have the opportunities that education and knowledge will provide. For your lessons, I have set aside the writings of Alexander Pope. If I am unavailable to read with you, I would like for you to copy such passages as you can find the time to do."

"I will do my best, Father. Mother has already shared some of Pope's works with me and I have picked my favorites. They are The Essays on Man. I am sure that I can keep myself occupied with these until you have more time."

"I knew I could count on you. Your mother has already given the younger ones a good start and you will be able to help them a lot as well."

That evening, working by the light of a glowing pine knot, John dipped his quill and began to write:

> *Epistle 1*
> *Essay on Man*
> *Argument*
> *Of the Nature and State of Man with Respect to the Universe*
> *Awake, my St. John! leave all meaner things*
> *To low ambition and the pride of kings.*
> *Let us ...*

In this exercise, perhaps, were planted the seeds of reasoning which would lead John into the career that would consume the greatest part of his life: the reasoning that would sharpen his judicial arguments and decisive thinking, shaping his future as a lawyer and ultimately leading to his appointment as Chief Justice of the United States.

Busy Father, Busy Family

THOMAS MARSHALL'S DUTIES as a justice of the peace and as surveyor of Fauquier continued to increase as the county grew. Although he believed fervently in his role as delegate to the House of Burgesses, it was a position that paid its members in honor and esteem. Friends like George Washington could afford to hold such positions since their family fortunes could support them. Thomas Marshall, however, could not afford this luxury. With his expanding family, Thomas decided with reluctance to resign as delegate in order to be able take on the better paying post of county sheriff from 1767 until 1769. He continued to stay abreast of all the latest colonial happenings, reading anything and everything that he could find. Again, the British Parliament was trying to tax the colonists on items such as glass, lead, paints, paper and tea. The colonists, in defiance, were refusing to buy any of them. Thomas Marshall followed these events with great concern.

The house in the hollow, which had seemed so large and spacious when the family first moved in, was rapidly filling up. The twins were toddling one-year-olds when sister Lucy was born. Now there were twelve in the house. Mother and Father's downstairs bedroom was always shared with the newest Marshall baby or babies. The loft upstairs was the scene of many giggling evenings when the older children were sent up to bed. At first Grandmother had the small room above Mother's and Father's room to herself and the children slept in the larger room to the west. Eventually, the older girls moved into Grandmother's room with her.

There was always a commotion going on. The toddlers babbled and cried and squealed and were into everything. Mother relied on Bett, Jenny, Esther and the two Hannahs to tend to these busy little babies. The family slaves also helped by preparing meals and doing many household chores. Their help allowed Mother the luxury of seeing to the children's education. Father was very pleased with the progress they were making. He had truly great ambitions for his oldest child, despite his limited time and his limited number of books. On several occasions, he had taken the opportunity to borrow some volumes from the extensive library of Lord Fairfax. But this was still not enough if Thomas Marshall wanted to assure his son the best possible education.

One evening, after he and John had finished reading together, he said, "John, I have just received a letter from the Reverend Archibald Campbell and he has agreed to take you on as a student at his academy. This is a wonderful opportunity for you. Campbelltown Academy is where George Washington and I went to school."

"But, Father, where is this academy? I know of none nearby."

"That's right. There aren't any nearby, that's why I've made these arrangements for you to go and study in Westmoreland County where I grew up."

"But, Father, isn't that far away? Will I have to leave you and Mother and the rest of the family? How will I get there? How long will I stay?"

"Just a minute, John. So many questions all at once. I'll try to answer them. Yes, you will have to leave here and stay at the academy. But I will travel with you to get you situated. I don't know how long you will stay. That will depend on many things and we will determine that as necessary. I know you will enjoy the wealth of learning that will be available to you at Rev. Campbell's."

"But, Father, you and Mother have always been able to provide for my education. Can't you continue to do so? Must I leave home?"

"I know this will be a big change, but I wouldn't do this if I didn't think it was important for you. My duties now afford me less and less time to work with you on your studies. Though I enjoy our time together you deserve more. I will miss having you here as much as you will miss being away. Try it for awhile and then we will see how long to continue."

John felt very uncertain about this. He'd never been away from his family before and now to be so far away and by himself. It was both frightening, but also exciting. That night John scarcely slept thinking about what lay ahead.

The day finally came when John was to leave. Father would take him to Campbelltown Academy on his way to Williamsburg where he was once again a delegate to the House of Burgesses. Mother had helped prepare his clothing and belongings for a year at school. Saying good-bye to the family was the most difficult part. John hugged each of his brothers and sisters. Eight-year-old Thomas tried to hide his tears at the thought of his big brother leaving, but wasn't very successful as he buried his face into John's side and clung to his waist. John had to pull him away and he tousled his hair, saying, "You be sure to practice throwing quoits while I'm away, so you can try to beat me when I return. I'll be back before you know it, Thomas." John was trying to convince himself as well as his little brother.

Finally, John stood before his mother as she looked him over and pronounced, "You look so grown up, John. I will miss you especially at lessons, but I know you will learn so many more things at Rev. Campbell's. When you return you will have to share all your new knowledge with me as well as with your brothers and sisters." Then she hugged him long and hard and John held back the tears that he could feel welling up inside. He knew his father wanted him to act like a man. But he wished that he didn't have to go so far away from his family and this place that he loved. He turned quickly, unable to speak because of the lump in his throat. He climbed up beside his father who was waiting in the carriage. Caesar was perched up front ready to drive away whenever Father gave him the word. He would be Father's attendant and see to his needs on this trip.

"All right, Caesar. We're ready now." As the carriage lurched forward, John turned and looked back until the house and his waving family disappeared from sight. Father put his arm around him and said, "I know this is difficult for you. But I also know that you will make us proud at the academy. If I didn't think it was important I wouldn't do this. Now sit back with me and watch as we pass through our beautiful countryside. You have seen Fauquier County, and now you will see some more of our Virginia colony. It is both a rich and important colony. Some day you will be proud to say this is your heritage." And with that father and son sat back in silence, enjoying the closeness of this shared moment.

Campbelltown Academy

THEIR HUNDRED-MILE JOURNEY took several days. John and his father stayed at inns and ordinaries along the way. As they traveled down into the neck of land between the Potomac and the Rappahannock Rivers, John saw tobacco plantations of some of the oldest aristocratic families of the colony, country that he was completely unfamiliar with. The stories Father told him about each of the large estates they passed fascinated him. Finally they pulled up at the gates of Campbelltown Academy. And here at the Academy he would attend school with the sons of some of these old and established Virginia families.

Rev. Campbell came to the entrance and shook hands with Father. After the two men exchanged greetings, Father said, "Rev. Campbell, I would like you to meet my oldest son, John. He is bright, enthusiastic and a good student. I know he will work his hardest while here at your academy. Your reputation for turning out students well-grounded in Latin and mathematics is legend. Your exacting standards will, I'm sure, make a tremendous impression on John." At the time, what his father said was merely words, but John would soon learn what "exacting standards" under the Reverend Archibald Campbell really meant.

John and the two men walked around the grounds of the academy. All too soon it was time for Father to be on his way. He still had some distance to travel before reaching Williamsburg. This was perhaps the hardest moment of all for John. His father gave him a quick hug. Then he stepped back and placed a hand on each of John's shoulders and said, "Make us Marshalls proud, John. Do your best and learn well."

After he climbed into his carriage and Caesar snapped the whip in the air sending the horses off down the road. As John watched his father, his best companion, depart, he felt more alone than he'd ever felt before. He would perhaps have stood there forever, except for the booming voice with a Scottish burr commanding, "Ther-r-re'll be no standing about, John Mar-r-rshall. Go to your-r-r-r-room and pr-r-repar-r-re for-r-r supper-r-r-r."

It was the Rev. Campbell and from the tone of his voice John knew that he had better do as he was told immediately.

John learned quickly that the Rev. Campbell ran a tight ship. In true Scottish fashion he believed in all work and no play in preparing boys to be astute and learned young men. John thought to himself, this was going to be a difficult time, particularly without the support and entertainment that his active and loving family had always provided for him. He walked toward his room, thinking how much he already missed the laughing and teasing of Elizabeth, Mary Ann, Thomas and his younger brothers and sisters. Just then he heard someone say, "You're new here, aren't you? My name is James. James Monroe. I'm just beginning here, too. It would be nice to have a friend to talk with. I'm not a resident student, but we would be able to study together during the day. Perhaps sometime you could come home with me for an evening."

John looked around at the smiling face of the boy by his side. Although younger than John by a couple of years, he reminded him of his brother, Thomas. And he did need a friend. Extending his hand, he said, "My name is John. John Marshall. I'm very glad to meet you, James Monroe," and the two boys shook hands. It was the beginning of their friendship, and their future careers would bring them together many times over the course of their lives.

Although there were boys of many ages at the academy, they all received the same basic instruction. The academy was small having only about twenty-five students. This assured them of a quality education. Each boy was pressed to achieve at his highest level. The new material and information being offered at the academy sparked John's eager thirst for knowledge. Latin especially excited John. It was new and he enjoyed the rote discipline it required. He had a quick mind and caught on fast. His mother and father had provided him with a firm basis in grammar from his study of Milton and Dryden. But it was his exercises with Pope's essays that had firmly planted the seeds for his future learning. John had memorized whole passages as he wrote, and he loved the precision of language that poetry presented. Latin presented that same precision of thoughts and words, and so John excelled in these studies.

Mathematics also interested John. In helping his father on surveying trips, John had needed to learn many basic arithmetic skills. So now it was simple to expand upon those. John was determined to learn as much as possible and as quickly as possible. In that way, he decided he would be able to return to The Hollow sooner.

Rev. Campbell expected his students to be prepared for every lesson and John and James worked together to be sure they were ready each day. The wrath of Rev. Campbell would come raining down like a torrent of hot coals upon any young man not prepared. John had seen one young student receive such a tongue-lashing during one of the first days of classes and had very quickly decided he never wanted to be at the receiving end of such a tirade. He worked to be a model student and to make his father proud.

Although the regimen was very strict, there was some time allowed for the boys to exercise their bodies as well as their minds. These were the times that John enjoyed the most. As one of the tallest boys at the school, and strong and muscular from his days of running and playing in the woods, he easily excelled in these areas. He always won the footraces and could out-jump everyone leaping over fences. Having learned early in life that humility is an important virtue, he was not boastful. This earned him the admiration of the other boys. His skill at quoits also continued to improve and he loved the relief such physical activity provided. But in spite of his successes at the academy, John longed more than anything to return home. Nothing was as wonderful as those times spent with his happy, noisy, loving family. He missed the gentle instruction of his mother, but most of all he missed the company of his father. Though he knew the Latin and mathematics that he was learning here were invaluable, nothing was more valuable to John than being at home.

When Father returned at the end of a year, John explained how he felt. His father listened attentively and said, "I am proud of your accomplishments here, John. Rev. Campbell has given me an excellent report on your conduct and your progress this year. The academy has been a wonderful opportunity, but perhaps I have a way for you to continue to learn at home. I think you will not need to return here next year. So, as soon as you say your farewells to your classmates and to Rev. Campbell we will be on our way back home."

That was the best news John had heard in a long time. He left his father and went to say good-bye to the other boys. He looked for his friend, James Monroe. Their friendship had helped John through a long and trying year. He found James sitting outside waiting for him and now getting up to greet him.

"James, good news. I am going home. Father is making new arrangements for my future studies, so I will not have to return." He watched James' smile melt away. He realized that James was sad to see him go. He hadn't thought about his friend missing him. Now John felt bad.

"I'm glad for you, John. I sure will miss having you to study with, but perhaps someday we'll meet again."

"I'm sure we will, James Monroe, I'm sure we will. You are a very good student and I know you have a great future ahead of you."

The two boys shook hands and James watched sadly as his friend walked away. John returned to the main building and shook hands with Rev. Campbell. Then he and his father climbed into their carriage and headed north.

Home at Last

THE COUNTRYSIDE looked more alive and vibrant to John than ever before. His dark eyes sparkled with delight. It was as though he were seeing it for the first time. The ride seemed to take forever and John thought they would never get home. Each night that they stopped at an inn seemed like an eternity. When the glorious Blue Ridge mountains finally appeared on the horizon, John realized just how much he had missed seeing them. At last, as they forded Goose Creek, John was perched on the edge of his seat, waiting impatiently to crest the hill. He knew that The Hollow and home would soon appear before him. When the carriage finally reached the top, John cried out, "Please, Father, stop the carriage! I want to get out and run the rest of the way!"

And that is just what he did. Leaping from the carriage, he raced as fast as his legs would carry him. All those days of racing with the boys at school were nothing compared to how fast his legs carried him on this course. He arrived at the door to the house before anyone had a chance to hear the carriage approaching. John burst through the door and swept the little ones up in his arms as he entered. He nearly scared them to death. Mother, knitting by the fire, stood up and dropped her basket of wool to the floor. John came over and hugged her long and hard. He kissed Grandmother on the cheek. By now all of his brothers and sisters had gathered around and were asking him questions and hugging onto his arms and legs. It was such a happy time. John felt like his world was finally back together again. He was amazed at how much each of the children had grown in a year. And, yes, there was another baby on the way. This would bring the number of children to ten, and thirteen living in the house in the hollow.

John didn't know what his father had meant when he said that he had an alternate source of instruction. At that moment he really didn't care about learning. He'd had a year of nothing but learning and now he just wanted to enjoy being part of his family again. He did share his papers and books and began to teach the older children some Latin and mathematics. It was fun to see them make faces at the strange sounding words he recited. Soon they were repeating, "*Amo, amas, amat, amamus, amatis, amant,*" as they conjugated Latin verbs. John pointed out the motto on Mother's family crest, *Veritas Vincit,* and now they learned that it meant "Truth Conquers". The older children were impressed by John's newly acquired knowledge and his parents were pleased at what he had accomplished.

John's father, in addition to all his other duties, had been appointed a vestryman of Leed's parish. As a vestryman, his duties included searching for and obtaining a new minister for the church they would establish. Thomas Marshall realized that this was an opportunity not only to set up the parish, but it also was a way to provide further education for his growing brood of children. He wrote to a friend in Edinburgh, Scotland asking him to find a young minister who would be willing to teach as well as to set up the church. When the friend finally responded he indicated that he was sure he had found just the sort of person Thomas Marshall was looking for. And so, not long after, a young man by the name of James Thomson arrived at The Hollow.

Since the newly formed parish of Leed's had only a tiny church which Thomas Marshall had helped to construct on North Cobbler Mountain, there really was no place for the young minister to reside. But John's father did not hesitate, for he had already decided that the new minister/teacher would live with his family at The Hollow. For James Thomson it was a roof over his head and good food, even though crowded and hectic. He, in turn, was a willing instructor for the older children who were eager learners.

Sleeping arrangements in the house were constantly changing. Alexander Keith, the latest newborn bearing Mother's family name, and two-year-old Lucy slept downstairs in Mother's and Father's room. Grandmother shared her smaller room in the loft with Elizabeth, Mary Ann, and Judith. John, young Thomas, James Markham, and the twins, William and Charles, shared the larger room of the loft. And it was here in the midst of these active and boisterous boys, ranging in age from four to fifteen, that the young and unsuspecting Scottish minister was situated. Many a night, Mr. Thomson found himself in the middle of a tickling war or settling a rousing pillow fight. Life at The Hollow was never dull.

The dining table in the main room was the scene of constant activity. When it was not used for eating at mealtimes, it was cleared and used as the classroom table. The children learned early in life how to block out the commotion going on around them and focus on their lessons. All at one time, there might be a baby crying, as well as little ones playing and singing in a corner, and the older children reciting Latin or reading Horace and Livy for Mr. Thomson. John loved all this activity though. After his year away at Campbelltown Academy, he never complained about the din.

One evening at dinner Father opened the discussion by announcing, "The Townshend Acts have finally been repealed. But it is most unfortunate that the killing of several Massachusetts colonists by British Redcoats had to occur first. They have taken to calling it "The Boston Massacre". Wouldn't you know though that Parliament still feels that they must

prove their point, and they are going to continue their tax on tea. So, as a result, we must continue to refuse to buy tea. I wonder what it will take before all of this stops?"

"It seems to me that the colonies must continue to stand together," Mr. Thomson offered. He enjoyed being included in these evening conversations

for they often provided inspiration for his Sunday sermons. "The British Empire is large and it is strong, but it is far away. If you are united in your stance, you may be able to finally get your way with Parliament."

"But, Father, isn't it dangerous to be so rebellious to the crown? If the Redcoats killed citizens in Boston, what is to keep them from using force throughout the colonies?" John asked.

"We have no guarantees, John. Perhaps, as Mr. Thomson suggests, we need to work together for our common good. Letters are being passed from one colonial legislature to another to try to keep us informed as to what is occurring in each of the colonies. I hope we will continue to keep this communication going. Meanwhile, we shall refuse to drink any English tea until the tax is lifted," Father replied.

"Thomas, we have been drinking herbal teas for so long now, I dare say we really won't miss it at all," Mother replied. "With Esther and Bett keeping our gardens growing so beautifully, we will continue to have plenty of soothing herbal teas for the entire family." "Although," Grandmother interrupted, "I must admit that on occasion I do miss a nice pot of my favorite breakfast tea. But don't worry. I wouldn't go against the boycott. It's just that I'd like it to end so I can have at least one cup of English tea before I'm too old to remember what it is like."

"Mother, I'm sure you will have your cup of fine tea soon. We must be patient and wait this out. The British tea merchants will not stand for this much longer. When the merchants lose money, they start to pressure Parliament for change. The situation has calmed down now, so we must just watch and wait."

One evening, Mr. Thomson stayed behind to speak alone with Father. He explained, "Sir, I truly would like to stay on as the minister of Leed's parish. I hope that you are pleased with my efforts in that respect. But if I am to take that position, I must return to England to receive my orders and official appointment. I hope that meets with your approval."

"Of course, I approve, James. We would like to have you here permanently. However, I must tell you that I know the children and Mrs. Marshall will miss you greatly. I wish you Godspeed and a quick return."

"Thank you, sir. I have thoroughly enjoyed my time here with you and your family. I am grateful for all your hospitality."

"James, it is I who am most grateful for the services that you have rendered both to our parish for- mation and to the education of my children."

John really was going to miss Mr. Thomson's lessons. What would he do now for instruction? The answer lay in his own thirst for knowledge. Armed with his father's books, and aided by his dictionary, he read and reread everything and anything he could find. He had always enjoyed reading his father's history books. But the volumes John appreciated the most turned out to be a set of books that his father brought home about the time that John turned sixteen.

A Wonderful Gift

RETURNING HOME from one of his trips to Williamsburg, Thomas Marshall set a large package, wrapped in paper and neatly tied with string, on the dining table. Calling John over, he said, "I had the opportunity to purchase something that might prove valuable for your further education. Go ahead and open it."

John quickly untied the string and peeled back the paper revealing four large volumes. He picked up the top heavy leather-bound book and carefully opened to the title page: *Commentaries on the Laws of England, Volume I, by Sir William Blackstone, American Edition.* The spines on the other books read *Volumes II, III,* and *IV.*

"Oh, Father, thank you. This is the most wonderful gift I have ever received. Now I will be able to learn everything about British law. Perhaps it will take me in a direction I never imagined. I want to begin reading them this very evening. Thank you, thank you, Father." Thomas smiled as his oldest son took the first volume, gathered up his trusted dictionary and sat down in a chair beside the fire and began to read. This was the son he knew was capable of great achievements. Watching him delve into the opening pages on the English legal system, he could imagine him arguing a case before some future court. Yes, John was capable of becoming a good lawyer. No, he could be a *great* lawyer. This was merely the first step. He knew in his heart that this was one purchase that would pay off many times over.

John spent all his free time reading through these four volumes. His dictionary was always there to help him when he came upon a new word or legal term he didn't understand. It was difficult reading, but John was determined, and he read it all and then he read it again. Yes, John thought, I definitely would consider being a lawyer.

1773

THE YEAR 1773 would prove to be pivotal in John's life. Several events would take place that would change the world around him. The first occurred when Thomas Marshall realized that the house at the hollow had reached its limits for his growing family, especially with child number eleven on the way. He had the opportunity to purchase 1700 acres of prime land only ten miles away from The Hollow. There he set about building a house that was befitting a man of his position in the community. It would be almost double the size of the The Hollow and have four rooms downstairs with huge fireplaces and chimneys at either end. The second floor would have three rooms with dormers and the largest upstairs room would have an additional fireplace. What he was most proud of was that this house would have real glass windows, one of the first in this area. The house was being constructed in a grove of oaks, so it would be called The Oaks, and eventually, Oak Hill. Since John had spent the best years of his life at The Hollow, this was not a move that he looked forward to. But he had no choice and he did realize that this larger house would be a better place for the whole family.

The next event in 1773 that would change the course of his life occurred far from The Hollow. In the spring of that year, with the boycott on English tea still in effect, the East India Company decided to try to sell several shiploads of tea at cheap prices in the colonies. New York colonists ran the ships out of their harbor, refusing to buy any tea on which they would have to pay a tax. The ships then sailed into Boston Harbor making the Massachusetts colonists equally unhappy. Late on a December evening, several colonists dressed as Indians sneaked aboard the ship and dumped the entire cargo of tea into the harbor. All this action so infuriated members of Parliament that they closed the port of Boston. The colonists called these the Intolerable Acts. This led to a meeting in Philadelphia in September, 1774 of delegates from the thirteen colonies which they called the First Continental Congress. By that fall the American Revolution had begun. As soon as militias began forming, Thomas Marshall and his son, John, were among the first to enlist. As members of the Fauquier Militia, they joined other units to become the

Culpeper Minute Men. They fought bravely in spite of many hardships in many of the battles for American independence.

Grandfather's Stories

"GRANDFATHER, GRANDFATHER! Wake up, wake up!"

The old man opened his eyes and looked into the rosy-cheeked face of his littlest granddaughter as she tugged on his sleeve. There was no denying that she was a Marshall. She had the same dark auburn hair he had had in his youth, and her dark eyes twinkled with the same mischievous delight.

"Grandfather, you've been sleeping so long, we thought you would never wake up. We want you to tell us your stories about the war and how you and your father fought with President Washington at Valley Forge."

John Marshall straightened himself in the chair.. Behind his granddaughter stood five or six of his other grandchildren looking at him with pleading eyes. The little girl continued, "You have so many good stories to tell, Grandfather, and we love to hear them over and over and over."

"All right, children, but you must sit quietly on the floor. Now, which story do you want to hear first?"

All the children began to shout at once.

"Tell about how you first met Grandmother Polly at Yorktown."

"No, tell about how you went to France on that special mission."

"I want to hear about how John Adams made you the Chief Justice and made Thomas Jefferson so mad."

"No! No! I think he should tell us about when he was little and lived at The Hollow."

The old man smiled. He'd just relived that story in his reveries. Yes, his boyhood days at The Hollow had been wonderful. As he looked around him he realized that he was a very lucky man. He had achieved many things in his lifetime that many men never even dream of accomplishing. His father and his mother had given him the education and opportunities to rise to the position he now enjoyed. His beloved wife Polly shared his life and gave him children that enriched his life, and, now, as he looked into the bright, eager faces of his grandchildren he knew how truly blest he was.

"Let me see, which story shall I tell you today?" he said as he stroked his chin thoughtfully, his dark eyes twinkling with delight. Then grinning broadly, he began, "My father and I were the best of companions, and we..."

BIBLIOGRAPHY

An Autobiographical Sketch by John Marshall. American Biography Series, Ann Arbor, MI, 1937.

Beveridge,Albert, *The Life of John Marshall, Vol. I, Frontiersman,Soldier,Lawmaker,1755-1788.* Houghton Mifflin Co., NY, 1916.

Baker,Leonard, *John Marshall: A Life in Law.* Macmillan Publishing, Co.,Inc., NY, 1974.

Dickinson, Josiah L., *The Fairfax Proprietary: The Northern Neck, the Fairfax Manors and the Beginnings of Warren County in Virginia.* Warren Press, VA, 1959.

Fauquier County, Virginia, 1759-1959. Fauquier County Bicentennial Committee, Warrenton, Virginia. Virginia Publishing, VA, 1959.

Fauquier County, Virginia Deeds, 1759-1788. Compiled by John K. Gott. Heritage Books, Inc., MD, 1988.

Feinberg, Barbara Silberdick, *John Marshall, The Great Chief Justice.* Enslow Publishers, Inc., NJ, 1995.

Foster,Frances B., *Old Homes and Families of Fauquier County, Virginia.* Virginia Book Company, VA, 1978.

Garraty, John A. and McCaughey, Robert, *The American Nation, A History of the United States.* Harper and Row, Publishers, Inc., NY, 1987

"The Genesis of Fauquier." Bulletin of the Fauquier County Historical Society, Vol. I, July, 1922.

"Germantown, Fauquier's First Settlement." News and Notes from the Fauquier Historical Society, Vol.30, Summer, 1981.

Groome, Harry C., *Fauquier During the Proprietorship: A Chronicle of the Colonization and Organization of a Northern Neck County.* Clearfield Co., MD, 1969.

Hobson, Charles R., *The Great Chief Justice: John Marshall and the Rule of Law.* University Press of Kansas, KS, 1996.

Hughes, Sarah S., *Surveyors and Statesmen, Land Measuring in Colonial Virginia.* The Virginia Surveyors Foundation, Ltd., and the Virginia Association of Surveyors, Inc., VA, 1979.

Kemper, Charles E., *"The Early Westward Movement of Virginia,1722-1734."* Virginia Magazine of History & Biography, Vol.13, 1906.

Magruder, Allan Bowie, *John Marshall.* AMS Press, NY, 1898.

Martha Washington's Booke of Cookery, transcribed by Karen Hess. Columbia University Press, NY, 1981.

Martin, Patricia Miles, *John Marshall*. Putnam, NY, 1967.

Martini, Teri, *John Marshall*. Westminster Press, PA, 1974.

Mason, Frances Norton, *My Dearest Polly, Letters of Chief Justice John Marshall to His Wife, with their Backgrounds, Political and Domestic, 1779-1831*. Garrett and Massie, Inc., VA, 1961.

Meade, Bishop William, *Old Churches, Ministers and Families of Virginia, Vol. II.* Genealogical Publishing Company, MD, 1966.

Monsell, Helen A., *John Marshall: Boy of Young America*. Bobbs-Merrill, IN, 1962.

Pope, Alexander, *The Poems, Epistles and Satires of Alexander Pope*. E.P.Dutton and Co. NY, 19—.

Russell, T. Triplett and Gott, John K., *A Historical Vignette of Oak Hill, Fauquier County Home of John Marshall, Chief Justice of the United States and Native Son of Fauquier County*. Willow Bend Books, MD, 2000.

Russell, T. Triplett and Gott, John K., *Fauquier County in the Revolution*. Willow Bend Books, MD, 1998.

Smith, Jean Edward, *John Marshall, Definer of a Nation*. Henry Holt and Company, NY, 1996.

Stephenson, Richard W. and McKee, Marianne M., *Virginia in Maps: Four Centuries of Settlement, Growth and Development*. The Library of Virginia, VA, 2000.

Stites, Francis N., *John Marshall: Defender of the Constitution*. Little, Brown and Co., MA, 1981.

The Tax Man Cometh, Land and Property in Colonial Fauquier County, Virginia: Tax Lists from the Fauquier County Court Clerk's Loose Papers, 1759-1782. Compiled by Joan W. Peters, C.G.R.S. Willow Bend Books, MD, 1999.

JOHN MARSHALL'S
BIRTHPLACE:

About one half mile southeast,
just across the railroad, a stone
marks the site of the birthplace,
September 24, 1755. He died at
Philadelphia, July 6, 1835.
Revolutionary officer,
Congressman, Secretary of State,
he is immortal as Chief Justice
of the United States Supreme
Court. During his long term of
office his wise interpretation of
the U.S. Constitution gave it
enduring life.

THE HOLLOW:

In 1765, John Marshall, then nine, moved with his family from his birthplace 30 miles southeast to a small, newly constructed frame house known as The Hollow.. The house built by his father, Thomas Marshall, was his home until 1773, when the family moved five miles east to Oak Hill. After the American Revolution began, Thomas Marshall and his sons, John Marshall, James Markham Marshall, and Thomas Marshall, Jr., fought in numerous Revolutionary War battles including Great Bridge and Yorktown. John Marshall later served as Chief Justice of the United States Supreme Court from 1801 to 1835.

OAK HILL
JOHN MARSHALL'S HOME:

Thomas Marshall, the father of future Chief Justice John Marshall, built Oak Hill about 1775 and relocated his family there from The Hollow, their former home nearby. John Marshall resided at Oak Hill for two years until he entered the Continental Army in 1775 at the age of twenty. He became the owner of the property in 1785 when his father moved to Kentucky. Although Marshall resided mostly in Washington, D.C., and in Richmond, he improved Oak Hill and used it as a retreat. In 1819 his son, Thomas, constructed an attached Classical Revival dwelling.

Present Day Fauquier County

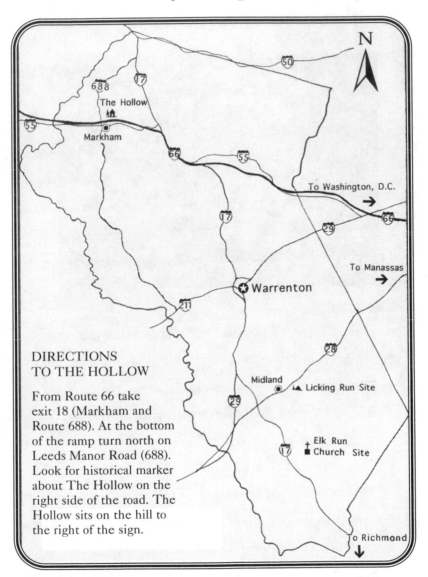

DIRECTIONS
TO THE HOLLOW

From Route 66 take
exit 18 (Markham and
Route 688). At the bottom
of the ramp turn north on
Leeds Manor Road (688).
Look for historical marker
about The Hollow on the
right side of the road. The
Hollow sits on the hill to
the right of the sign.

About the Author

A native of New York state, Geraldine {Jeri} Susi spent some of her grade school years near California's Mojave Desert but returned east to attend high school in Northern Westchester County. She won a prize in New York State's Year of History Contest celebrating its 350th anniversary and was graduated as salutatorion of her class.

She completed two years at Elmira College before she married Ron Susi, then a second Lieutenant in the Air Force. In 1965 she received her Bachelor's degree in Texas. The marriage would eventually take them to every state either on vacation or in service. Each of their four children was born in a different state. In Alabama the family stayed long enough for the mother to receive her Master's degree as a reading specialist, and in 1973 she became Air University's nominee for Air Force Wife of the Year.

After moving from sunny Alabama to snowy Michigan, the whole family won contests in ice sculpturing. They enjoyed skiing and snowmobiling too. When Colonel Susi was transferred to the Pentagon the family settled in their own house in Burke, Virginia; and Mrs. Susi began teaching for Fairfax County at Lemon Road Elementary, Cherry Run Elementary, Longfellow Intermediate, and finally Lees Corner Elementary. Her love of children, history and writing inspired her to write the popular book of fiction for fourth- to seventh-graders entitled LOOKING FOR PA: A Civil War Journey fron Catlett to Manassas.

She interrupted her work on a sequel to that story to write this book about the boyhood of America's famous Supreme Court Justice John Marshall who was appointed Chief Justice in 1801. Marshall's home, The Hollow, still stands and is now being restored. It is located not far from where the Susis built their permanent home after the children had gone off to college. Now retired, the Susis share their continuing travels, sports and creative art projects with all the family—including seven grandchildren.